The Magic Driver

The Magic Driver

Jason T. Ross

Illustrated by Benedict Rullan

CURIOUSLY CRUISING PUBLISHING
SEATTLE, WA

The World Golf Adventures of Justice and Gigi:
The Magic Driver

Copyright @ 2011 Jason T. Ross

Library of Congress Control Number: 2011924903

ISBN 978-0-615-45844-1

Edited by Geoff Pope and Michael Orbeck

Cover art by Benedict Rullan

Printed in the United States of America

To my wife,

"I walked amongst the calmness of the sand,

meditating in her unconscious purity--

content with the idea that eternity exists."

-JRS

CHAPTER ONE

*T*he crimson evening sun crept back over the horizon. Its rich colors were fading into an animated dream, blending into intricate swirling patterns. The remaining sunrays fought to stay awake as they streamed through the quiet clouds, highlighting the contrast of green on the fairway that lay restlessly ahead. The air was still, and the gallery stood like loyal soldiers, anticipating the next tee shot that could determine a new junior golf champion at the Annual Cougar Classic.

Justice was poised and confident standing over his scraped Spreeline ball. The pressure was only on Brady Locker, Justice's obnoxious rival, and the winner of the previous three local tournaments. Brady was the neighborhood bully and rather skilled at the job. When he wasn't winning golf tournaments, he spent his time egging cars from the roof of his three-story house and unleashing his ugly Rottweiler on unsuspecting bystanders. Brady, or "Brady the Lady" as he was commonly referred to at school, was slightly pudgy, heavily freckled, and unfortunately the son of a former golf pro. Brady received private lessons, the latest Zipgroove golf clubs, and all the new high-tech gear on the market--basically everything a spoiled brat could ever need. He had been untouchable in the junior golf circuit…until now. Justice shifted his eyes to the focal point on his ball, clenched his teeth, and ripped a 250-yard drive on the par 4, 18th hole, that had destiny written all over it. It faded left to right, and settled in the middle of the fairway.

"I could make that shot blindfolded!" heckled Brady as he got ready to tee off himself.

They were both two under through the first seventeen holes. Brady had a three-shot lead until the debacle on the 14th hole, where his ball found the water hazard on his drive. The Cougar Classic was being held at the Spann Lake Golf Course for the fourth year in a row. There were several holes that had a high risk/reward ratio, and the 14th was one of them. A cluster of trees at 220 yards divided the fairway in half. Brady's machismo got the best of him when he attempted to loft it over the tall branches. When it ricocheted off the far left tree and trickled into the pond below, Justice knew he had a chance. He decided to lay up instead of going for the glory on this difficult hole, and that may have made all the difference. The Spann Lake Golf Course had the most scenic views in the state. Mt. Rainier could be seen from almost every vantage point, and on a clear day you could practically see the powdered snow cascading down its slopes.

It all came down to this final 18th hole, where Justice had the momentum on his side. Brady placed his ball on his bright orange golf tee. His swing was tense, his shoulder not getting its full rotation. His ball drifted wearily, slicing to the right, into the intermediate rough, thirty yards behind Justice's ball.

"Nice try, big shot!" exclaimed Gigi, Justice's little sister and his caddy for the tourney. Gigi had a bubbly personality and wasn't afraid to speak her mind. Her bright red shoelaces, wavy brown pigtails and petite stature made her appear less than threatening, but Justice knew otherwise. She was a five-foot ball of sassiness and was considered a tomboy by most of her peers. She and Justice made the perfect team and they had been playing together since she was three, almost seven years ago. Justice had recently celebrated his 12th birthday, and he made sure she never forgot who was older. They were great friends, even though their personalities were polar opposites. Justice was calm and extremely shy, and you would never catch him bragging about his golf prowess. Tall and lanky, Justice towered to nearly 5'9", with small facial features resembling a stretched-out gummy bear with light brown frizzy hair. His clothes hung loosely on his wiry frame and his favorite soiled Colts hat fit like a glove on his head.

Their mother had been born in the Philippines and their father was born and raised in Mansfield, Washington, so they sported a year-round tan.

"I see your ball, Brady boy," taunted Gigi. "You should have brought a chainsaw with you. That spruce tree doesn't look like it's moving anytime soon."

Brady grabbed his top-of-the-line 4 iron and tried to punch it out, wanting to avoid the looming tree that was cemented only a couple feet from his dirt-crusted ball. *Whack!* He got nice contact--and even a better roll. His ball was resting on the front edge of the vast, rolling green.

"How do you like that shot, losers?"

Justice ignored him and pulled out his rusty

6 iron. He got his old set of clubs at Skeeter's Thrift Store. They were all his ten-dollars-a-week allowance could afford, but he loved them all the same. The 6 iron had the best grip on it of the set, but it was rusted over and the grooves were nearly worn out. It felt like an old friend in his hand as he gripped it tightly.

"Come on, Justice, all you have to do is hit the green and you can de-throne this little monster," said Gigi.

Knees wobbling, Justice swung swiftly through his ball, catching it in the sweet spot on his grooveless iron. It got a good flight, and travelled effortlessly to the two-tiered lush green ahead, sitting with an uphill putt. A cheer erupted from the gallery, followed by Justice's patented fist pump. He could almost see the finish line. He walked nonchalantly toward the green, taking in a deep sigh of relief. A 6-foot putt with a little break is all Justice had left to be crowned the new Cougar Classic champion. Brady's hasty chip shot landed well short of the pin, leaving him a 20-foot miracle putt with a severe break. His attempt was a feeble one, as the ball blew past the hole. The spotlight shined down solely on Justice and the six feet he faced to the pin.

"Breathe. You've made this putt a hundred times," encouraged Gigi.

His putter shook so bad that it looked like a jack hammer at warp speed. He exhaled slowly and then heard the sweetest sound of his life-- *clunk*, his ball finding the bottom of the cup.

"It's in!!! You won!!!" yelled out Gigi. Overwhelmed by emotion, Justice let out a single tear, rolling down his frosty cheek as Gigi bear-hugged him until he almost passed out. Brady stormed off the green, kicking over his clubs and throwing a temper tantrum like a three-year-old.

"I'm so proud of you, Justice! You finally shut Brady the Lady up. It's a wonderful sound of silence!"

The trophy was presented by Fredrick Gesser, a legend in the PGA, and a native to the Emerald City. The trophy was huge, making it look like the Empire State Building compared to the little collection Justice had on his dusty shelf at home. The shiny silver around the cup was practically blinding him, and most importantly the word "Champion" was engraved in large cursive letters at the base.

"I can't believe this, Gigi. This is the biggest trophy I've ever seen!"

"You deserve it, big brother. Now you're on your way to catching up with my trophy case."

The celebration lasted awhile. He wanted to shake as many hands as possible, and be the polite victor.

"Come on, Justice," Gigi said, "let's get out of here. I'm getting dizzy from all these people smothering us."

"Me too. Hey, I know a short cut through the second fairway. We'll be out of here in no time."

The two of them walked off, waving at the crowd as they made their escape. Justice was holding his trophy like it was a newborn baby seeking warmth in his arms.

CHAPTER TWO

"Y ou played well, young man, a real
fighter," came a raspy voice from
behind a large spruce tree.

Startled, Gigi asked, "Where is that voice
coming from?"

"That sure is some trophy you got there!"

The man was old and weathered. His
clothes were wrinkled, but looked very fancy. His

head rested against the tree, his white beard stubbles as thick as the bark on the spruce. He had olive skin and spoke with a slight accent.

"Oh, thank you sir," answered Justice.

"Don't call me sir, young man. My name's Kuya, Kuya Palmer."

Justice drew back, scared and weary of this old man.

"I've played in a dozen tournaments but never won any kind of trophy--came close once in Hawaii, though."

He continued, coughing in between words.

"I got sick a few years ago, lost my swing and my ambition to play. My only wish was to have a trophy. So I applaud you, champ."

Gigi interjected, "Kuya, we should be going home now. Our dad is expecting us."

She nudged Justice and motioned her head toward the course's exit. Justice was holding his trophy straight out from his side and gesturing towards the old man.

"Kuya, I would like you to have this trophy. I want your wish to come true."

"That's very generous of you son, but you earned it, and I couldn't possibly take that away from you. Thanks anyway."

"Are you crazy?" remarked Gigi. "I think your brains got scrambled back on the 18th hole. Let's get out of here."

Justice turned again to the old man. "No, I'm serious. Here, take it. I will beat that Brady character again anyways. I can get another one, no big deal." Then he handed the championship trophy to the old man.

Kuya wilted into his own hands, his emotions overcoming him. He looked up towards the sky, his eyes practically swelling with disbelief.

"That is the most generous thing anybody has ever done for me. God bless you, young man."

After a pause, he said, "Now, I would like to give you something."

From behind the spruce tree, the old man grabbed what looked like a crooked fishing pole with a warped head on it. The shaft was chipped to shreds, and the rubber on its dirty white handle was barely clinging on.

"This is my lucky driver, and it has taken me all over the world. Ever since I became sick, I've been searching for someone worthy enough to pass it down to. You have a genuine heart, young man, and I believe you are the chosen one."

Justice accepted the driver, looking curiously at his new gift.

"It doesn't look like much, but it is strong and fierce like a lion, its teeth gnarling, like the predator that it is. To bring out its fiercest strength," Kuya continued, "close your eyes and imagine something pure and close to your heart, Justice. Its powers are vast, so please use caution. Once you have left, you must seek out only the most remote and exclusive courses to use the driver on, to continue your journey. I bless you two on the adventures that await you."

They all said their uncomfortable farewells as Gigi and Justice strode across the darkening fairway.

"That sure was bizarre," said Justice.

"You're telling me! What a crazy old guy."

"Well, perhaps we could go fishing tomorrow and try out your new driver," giggled Gigi.

"Good idea. I'll bring the worms and lures."

It was about a mile walk back to their house from the course. They lived in a cul-de-sac in a three-bedroom rambler. It was by far the ugliest house on the block--painted lime green, looking like a gigantic Tic Tac candy with grated windows, and a poorly constructed porch. The backyard was laced with weeds, lined with blackberry bushes as sharp as barbed wire. It was connected to a hiking trail that led to a small pond where they used to go fishing when they were younger. The pond was covered with lily pads, and they would often hear the frogs chatting away at night.

They were raised by their dad mostly, as their mom Regina was hardly ever around, this time being no exception. She owned a small struggling bakery in town, and she practically lived there. The bakery was called Regina's Sweet Delights, specializing in meringue pies and designer cupcakes. Justice and Gigi always looked forward to their birthday parties, where they could devour their mom's latest creations.

Their dad Peyton was asleep on the couch, the TV flickering on an old episode of the *Wheel of Fortune.*

"I can't wait to tell Dad about my victory."

"We'll catch him in the morning. I don't want to wake him up; you know how cranky he gets when he's tired."

"Good point. I'm so sleepy, sis. I'm going to grab a snack and head to bed. My feet are killing me."

"Night night, big bro. I enjoyed watching you destroy Brady the Lady finally!"

"The pleasure was all mine."

Justice went to his room, lay down in his rickety bed and was greeted by Rocky, his spoiled rotten calico cat that never left his side. She snuggled on his chest and was gently pawing his face, as she often did. The night sky dimmed as visions of the day's victory ran through Justice's mind. The crescent moon peeked in through the window, its silhouette rested on the contours of his new driver and slowly drifted away into a myriad of stars.

CHAPTER THREE

"Come on, sleepy head," said Gigi. "Let's play the short nine at Cecil Greens. I'm itching to beat you again. I'll even give you a couple strokes."

"Wishful thinking, sis. You can count this champion in."

"Yeah, yeah," Gigi smirked back.

"Let's sneak out the backyard. We can be

back before Dad wakes up."

This was their normal routine when they wanted to play a quick round. Peyton couldn't ever see the point of spending so much money on green fees and fancy clubs. They failed to tell him that they worked out a deal with the maintenance crew at Cecil Greens, where they help repair the divots in the fairway, and then they can play for free a few times a month during the dew sweeper time.

It was about eight blocks down the street to the executive course, and they arrived shortly after a brisk walk. It was much breezier today than during the tournament. The leaves were blowing in the swirling wind, and the dew on the first tee box was crunchy and partially frozen. This is the greatest feeling for Justice and the reason why he always bears the cold and often rainy conditions to play--becoming entranced in a green blur of fairways and undulating greens, pressing the pause button on life's trials, adrenaline pumping through his veins, while anxiety escapes through every pore. Nothing can top this feeling--nothing!

"Ok champ, I'll let you have the first honors. Don't be nervous. Not like it matters that you're going to lose again to your little sister!"

Justice grabbed his old 3 wood, which he is basically automatic with.

"Hey scaredy pants, why don't you try that fishing pole now," mocked Gigi. "I can see the trout jumping up ahead."

"Ok, I will, but don't laugh too hard if I land on my tush trying to swing it. The grip is as slick as a stick of sweet cream butter."

Justice took a couple practice swings and prepared to give it a whack.

"Don't forget to think of something pure and close to your heart," teased Gigi.

Justice did just that, closing his eyes, concentrating intensely, and swung down and hit his ball square off the tee. The contact sound was deafening; a high pitched screeching noise came off the club, like the sound of a train stopping on its tracks. His hands became tingly, numbness filled his legs, his mind went blank. The sky opened up above, and the statues of morning clouds drifted and crumbled.

The leaves began wrestling more vigorously, chasing each other in a circular motion, like a merry-go-round that had a turbine engine. The fall colors were mixing rapidly, creating a collage that painted the tee box, which was now...deserted. Justice and Gigi disappeared into the fierce wind as quickly as the fall collage was drawn. Remnants of their voices were present, laughing amongst the stillness of the morning.

CHAPTER FOUR

*T*he waves crashed melodically against the
narrow shoreline. The tips washed over
the crystallized white sand, white as Santa's beard
and fine like salt sprinkled over a ballpark pretzel.
The sand was scorching hot, matching the
sweltering heat that engulfed the beach. Sweat was
dripping off Justice and Gigi's faces. They looked
out into the turquoise sea, shades of blue
becoming darker as the sea left its shallow
confines.

"Umm, Justice," Gigi, in a daze, murmured. "How come we're not at Cecil Greens? Did I already beat you?"

"I have no idea. I became tingly and my ears started ringing. Can't recall anything that happened afterwards."

"What's going on then?" asked Gigi.

"Beats me. All I remember is teeing off with…"

"Oh my goodness, the new driver! Are you kidding me, that crazy old man was right!"

"This is nuts. Maybe we're only dreaming, sis?"

"Ouch! What was that for?" Justice asked, grimacing in pain.

"I gave you a lobster pinch, just to make sure. So, yes this is very real."

"Hey Justice, what was your pure thought anyway? You know, before you swung that fishing pole of yours."

"I was thinking of the time when Dad took us to Ruby Beach in the Olympics. Remember the little Dungeness sea crab that pinched you? You cried for like an hour. That was one of my favorite trips of all time."

"Well, that explains it, and now we're sitting on some beach and it feels like a thousand degrees outside."

"I wonder where we are. It sure doesn't feel like home."

The beach was virtually empty, except for a young girl who was approaching them, humming quietly, and kicking up the sand as she walked. She was as short as Gigi, her skin really tan and her hair jet black, with a small white bow in it.

"*Sa-wat-dee ka,*" said the little girl.

"*Sa-bai dee mai?*" she attempted again.

"I mean hello, how are you? You don't speak Thai?"

Gigi answered curtly, "Thai? Why would we speak Thai?"

"Because you're in Thailand, silly, that's why."

"Excuse me, what did you say?" Gigi asked, stunned.

"Thailand--the land of smiles in the heart

of Southeast Asia, on the great Phi Phi Don Island, to be exact," replied the girl.

The weight of the world hit Justice and Gigi right smack in the mouth. They both looked over at each other and glanced at their surroundings once again. They weren't sure how or why, but they were standing on a beach they couldn't pronounce, their shoes practically melting, somewhere in Thailand!

"Say, why do you two have your golf clubs with you, and are wearing golf shoes? This is a small island. There's no golf here."

"Uh...we were only...you know, we really like golf," stuttered Justice.

"I guess so. It's a little strange though. My name is Bussra, by the way. I live here on Phi Phi Island."

"I'm Gigi, and this is my older brother Justice. We're from Seattle."

"Where?"

"It's a city on the West Coast, in America."

"Wow, how cool. You're a long way from home! So which hotel are you staying at? Maybe we can hang out later?"

"We aren't staying anywhere yet. We just got here."

Actually, we'd like to get back to dry land if that's possible?"

"Sure, there's only one way off this island, and that's by long-tail boat. She pointed to an empty boat right near the shore. It was white with green trim. The paint had chipped off a little bit on the sides. It was like an elongated canoe, about ten meters long, with a single motor that weighted the back end enough to have the nose stick out of the water.

"That's my uncle's boat. He built it himself years ago from an old palm tree. I'm a pretty good driver too. Let me tell my mom and then I can give you a ride if you'd like?"

She ran back to her modest red house near the beach, and returned shortly with a few bottles of water her mom had given her. The three of them hopped on the long-tail boat. Justice hauled their clubs into the storage cubby while Bussra used a huge bamboo pole to shove off from the shallow shore.

"Ok, hold on Americanos, these boats are pretty fast. I wouldn't want to lose one of you. We just met," laughed Bussra.

"You sure live on a beautiful island, Bussra," said Justice.

"Phi Phi Don is fantastic. It's known for its double bay. Just like an hour glass. It gets kinda boring at times, being such a small place. My family owns a little restaurant in town. We have the best *tom yum goon* in Thailand! I help out in the kitchen when I'm not in school."

"*Tom yum goon?*"

"It's Thailand's signature soup. It's very spicy and includes shrimp, fish and vegetables. It's *aroy mak*! That means super good! I'll get you some later, when we stop for lunch."

"I was planning to take you to Phuket Beach. You can get back home from there, but before I do, I want to take you to my favorite beach in Southern Thailand--Maya Bay. It's only five kilometers away."

"Kilometers?" asked Gigi puzzlingly.

"Oh yeah, you don't use the metric system too much in America. About three miles then, right across the Andaman Sea."

"Sure, we might as well. Don't have any plans anyway."

Justice and Gigi sat back in this stretched canoe, gripping the sides firmly until their knuckles turned white, enjoying the warm breeze coming off the boat, accompanied by the light spray of water. Their initial fears of not being home were slowly floating away in the warm, splashing sea. After about a twenty minute boat ride, they arrived at the entrance of the bay.

"Hey guys, we're here--Maya Bay. It's still pretty early, so we'll have plenty of time to enjoy the beach."

Their jaws dropped as they gazed around the inlet and could see the most serene, crystallized white sandy beach and palm trees ever imaginable. The bay was surrounded by sheer limestone cliffs, and the seagulls flew carelessly overhead. Bussra turned off the engine, and they drifted across the very shallow, turquoise water that acted as a looking glass to all the tropical fish below.

"Hey sis, look at all those colorful fish and corals."

"The last time I saw so many fish, we were at Jack's Fish House, and they were on the menu," laughed Gigi.

"Say, do you two want to get a closer look? I think my uncle might have some extra snorkel masks somewhere in the boat."

"That would be sweet! We've never been snorkeling before, it looks difficult," replied Justice.

"No way, it's easy. I'll help you, don't worry, ok."

The boat practically drifted right up to the beach on its own. They all got out and helped pull the boat up onto the shore. The beach itself was small, and the forest went back as far as the eye could see. The water was calm as the limestone cliffs blocked the wind from entering the bay. This was the most tranquil and beautiful place the two had ever seen, and that included all those tropical beaches they showed on the travel channel back home. They were staring out at a real life mosaic, listening to it breathe and taking in the vastness of its purity.

"Hey, I found them! And he had some extra fins too. Here you go. They should fit you." Bussra tossed a couple of snorkel masks to Gigi and Justice and assisted putting them on correctly.

"Ok, so when you get in the water, just breathe in and breathe out slowly through the snorkel tube and kick with the fins."

Bussra was the first to jump in the water, followed by Gigi and then Justice. They swam out a ways and looked down at the red coral. There were so many different kinds of tropical fish, it was difficult to follow only one. The fish seemed subdued and not bothered by the three masked intruders who were floating above their home.

"Hey guys, let's swim out a little further. I think I see a school of Clownfish. They're my favorite."

"I see them too, swimming near that huge white coral," replied Justice.

"Ok, hold your breath on the count of three. We're going to dive down and swim with them. One...two...three."

They all took a deep breath and turned upside down as they plummeted into the depths of the bay, like little ducks fetching their first meal. The Clownfish were incredible looking. They were small and aerodynamic, with bright orange blotches covering a black and grey body. They were moving in rhythm with the three visitors, going in and out between their fins and at times nibbling at their legs. Gigi spotted another colorful fish, which also swam alongside the three. Justice was practically turning blue from holding his breath so long, so they all decided to resurface for some air.

"There's like another entire world in this bay," commented Gigi.

She turned to Bussra and asked, "What was that heavily scaled yellow fish swimming beside us?"

"I believe it was a Titan Trigger fish, but be careful-- they have a tendency to bite; and when the Trigger bites you, it's gonna hurt!"

"On that note, let's start heading back before it gets hungry for American food. Besides, my legs feel like they ran 30 miles," said Gigi.

They reached the shore and lay on their backs, soaking in the bright morning sun and letting their legs touch the tepid seawater.

"That was awesome!" exclaimed Justice.

"Yeah, Thailand is an excellent place to go snorkeling and scuba diving, especially down here in the Andaman Sea. It's one of the very best in the world. My older brother Johann loves to go diving nearby at Loh Samah Bay. He always sees giant sea turtles and moray eels when he dives at night. Johann is certified and everything. Scuba diving takes lots of practice, but well worth it, he says."

"If we're lucky, we might even see a shark on the way out. Don't worry--they are only Leopard sharks, harmless."

"Sharks, hungry Trigger fish--I think that's my signal to exit this place," said Justice.

"I guess we can start heading back towards Phuket. It will take us about an hour and a half."

Bussra pushed off with the bamboo pole again and slowly floated back toward the mouth of Maya Bay. The sun was beating down stronger as the afternoon was slowly approaching. Justice and Gigi felt a little braver now, and they were dangling their toes off the edge of the long-tail boat, trying to get a bigger splash of sea mist to cool them down. They eagerly took in the sights on the jaunt across the sea.

CHAPTER FIVE

"So, here we are guys. This is Karon Beach, part of Phuket. There are three main beaches all close together--Karon, Kata, and Patong, and this one's my favorite."

"Grab your clubs, and let's get some lunch. I'm so hungry!"

This beach was much busier than the one at Phi Phi Island. There were dozens of hotels, restaurants and vendors selling everything you could imagine. It was a lively atmosphere and they found a quaint restaurant right near the beach and sat down at an outside table. The waiter poured them some water and took their order.

"Let's try some *gairng kee-ow waan*--green curry, and *tom yum goon*," suggested Bussra.

The waiter asked politely, "*Pet mai?*"

"That means *spicy*. Think you can handle a little fire?" added Bussra.

"Sure, maybe a tad spicy is ok," answered Justice. "My dad makes a mean spicy burrito back home, so I'm used to the heat."

When the food came and Justice tried a couple bites, his face turned as red as the stoplight that swung in the wind on the street corner.

"You ok, big brother. Should I call the fire department?"

"Thai food is known to be extremely spicy and very flavorful. You know what they say: the hotter the country, the hotter the food," Bussra chimed in.

Justice was dripping like a leaky faucet,

grabbing all the glasses of water off the table and gulping them down, one at a time.

"So, Bussra, I was wondering how come your English is so good? You speak just as well as a lot of my friends back home," asked Gigi.

"Oh thanks, what a compliment! Well, my dad made me study English with a private tutor, ever since I could walk. Thais take great pride in learning your difficult language."

After the filling lunch, they decided to take a walk around the crowded beach.

"Hey guys, the best way to cruise the beach is by moped. Let's rent a couple over there. My friend Narate is working today, and he never charges me. You can drive one, can't you?"

"Oh sure, no problem--can't be much different than my push scooter back home," said Gigi.

They mounted these awkward bikes and Narate gave them some quick driving tips.

"Ok, go slow and don't forget to put on your helmet. These bikes scratch easily, and so do tourists, so try not to crash them," he said jokingly.

"Let's take a trip up to Patong Beach. It's a steep and winding road, but lots of fun to drive fast!" Bussra said excitedly.

Justice was the last one to take off and also the slowest. He was using the hand gears erratically, jolting himself back and forth. First, he would zoom ahead and then come to a screeching stop. The gears were taking him some time to get used to, and the constant whiplash was getting old fast.

"Easy, Justice. This isn't your video game Motor Cross Derby that you think you're so good at."

"I know. This is ten times scarier!"

They cruised along Karon Beach, looking out at the invigorating sea that first captivated them. Gigi's hair was flying, leaving a trail of dark brown and wavy streaks in the air. She pretended she was one of Charlie's Angels on a top-secret mission. The only thing missing were her aviator sunglasses she often sported when trying to impress the boys in her class.

They stopped atop a cliff and gazed out again at the open sea. The seagulls were playing tag above, hovering in the slight breeze.

"We've been having so much fun, I almost forgot to ask where you are trying to get to?" asked Bussra.

"I guess we should be getting home soon. Where do the planes fly out of?"

"All the international flights fly out of Bangkok, Thailand's capital, and biggest city. It's about twelve hours from here by bus. The best way is to fly from Phuket. It's only about an hour from there."

Justice nudged Gigi and whispered, "We have no idea how to get home. We can't take a plane with no money."

"Ok, smarty pants, do you want to tell her that we magically appeared here after hitting your new driver?"

"Good point. Well, if the driver got us here, it should be able to get us out. But we need to use it on a remote course, remember?"

Gigi turned to Bussra, looking a little

frazzled.

"Bangkok will be great, and I guess it would be fun to play on a nice, remote golf course before we go."

"*Remote?* I'm not too sure about that, there are over a hundred wonderful golf courses throughout Thailand. Take your pick."

"Great. That really narrows it down. We're doomed," said Gigi.

"Hey, I have an idea. My dad's best friend and old college roommate lives in Phuket Town, not too far from here. He used to own a biplane that he fixed up back when he was an airline mechanic. It's worth a shot."

"I guess we could try. What do you mean *fixed up?*" asked Justice.

"Don't worry. It's a short flight to Bangkok. It doesn't need to last long," laughed Bussra. "So come on, let's get going. We need to get to the monkey park in the mangrove forest before they close."

"Monkey park?" asked Justice and Gigi simultaneously.

"That's where Hedgie works. He's the head monkey trainer at the new facility. He teaches the young monkeys to ride bicycles and dance to salsa music."

"Now, I think I've heard everything!" exclaimed Gigi.

CHAPTER SIX

*T*hey mounted their mopeds and continued on the narrow road, reaching the top of the steep hill before driving into Phuket Town. Bussra was putting the pedal to the metal and Justice still lagged behind. His arms were shaking, and he was shedding skin trying to hold on to the vibrating handlebars. They rode awhile longer until they reached a dirt path.

"It might be a little bumpy, so drive slow and try to avoid all the potholes," said Bussra.

They hesitantly continued down the road, the dirt kicking up from the back of Bussra's moped, leaving a small coat of dirt and grime on Gigi's face. The road seemed to go on forever. Five kilometers of dirt and uncertainty, then the mangrove forest appeared in the distance. Mangroves are woody trees that look as if they grew on stilts. They play house to hundreds of species of animals in the wetlands and are said to be the rainforest by the sea.

There was a clearing up ahead, with a few bamboo trees off to the right, and Gigi noticed one of the trees were moving. They parked their mopeds for a moment to watch.

"Hey, look. That guy is kicking that bamboo tree, wiggling it back and forth. You think he needs some help chopping it down?" asked Gigi curiously.

"Haha. You're hilarious, girl! He's doesn't want to chop it down. He's practicing Muay Thai kick boxing. It strengthens his shins, so he can be a stronger fighter."

"Well, I don't know what that tree ever did to him, but it sure looks pretty painful."

After a good laugh, they took off down the path and finally got to the gate, which was marked by two gigantic monkeys carved in stone. But they were too late, the park was closed.

"Oh no, we must have just missed it," said Justice.

"Follow me. I know another way in."

They rode along the side of the park until they came across a break in the wooden fence. They had to get off the mopeds and push them through the tiny opening. They stood in the center of the pathway in the monkey park, surrounded by mangroves and the most remarkable sight. Thousands of little monkeys were sitting in the trees. They looked like furry moss on the mangroves with white teeth and beady, mischievous eyes poking out. The monkeys were literally everywhere. The three kids started walking their mopeds down the path, now covered with fur and wagging little tails. The red carpet of monkeys appeared to be welcoming them, when they were startled by a Thai voice up ahead.

"Hey kids, the park is closed. Didn't you see the sign?" yelled a man walking down the path.

Bussra put her hands together to form a tiny speaker, and replied in English. "Hedgie, is that you?"

"Yes, how do you know my name?"

"It's me, Bussra Tongtu. You went to school with my dad."

"Oh, hi. You sure have grown since the last time I saw you. What are you doing here?"

Hedgie was heavy set with rounded dimples and not much taller than 5'6". He was nicknamed Hedgie in secondary school, on the account he looks like a hedgehog. He spoke with a heavy accent, but slow enough that he was still understandable. He had a long braided goatee that was matted just like his curly black hair that peeked out from his tan safari hat. His overalls were dark blue with monkey patches all over it.

He had bulging eyes and extremely thick eyebrows.

"These are my friends from America, and they're trying to get to Bangkok. Do you still happen to have that old biplane?" asked Bussra.

"I do, but haven't flown it for years. It's still in good shape, but might need a little work to get it going again."

"So you broke into my monkey park and want to borrow my plane? You are as tenacious as your dad. Like father, like daughter," laughed Hedgie.

"Can you, pleeeeeeeeeeeease?" begged Bussra.

"Ok sure, on two conditions. First, you will stay at my place tonight, and I will make you a special Thai dinner. Second, I want to practice my English with your friends."

Gigi busted in: "Oh thank you, thank you. We would be glad to help."

"I never understood American slang too well."

"It's as easy as pie, no worries," said Gigi.

"Huh?"

"I see I have my work cut out for me. . . I mean, it would be fun to teach you a few slang words," she chuckled.

The monkeys quickly started gathering around them. Before they could blink, there were about a hundred little fur balls that covered the entire pathway. Hedgie walked over to Justice and made a clicking sound with his teeth. Suddenly a scraggly black and white monkey jumped on Justice's shoulder, and started tapping him like a drum.

"Justice, I think you finally found your long lost twin brother!" giggled Gigi.

"Hey, what's he doing?" asked Justice.

"Don't worry, they're all friendly. He's only saying hello," said Hedgie.

Gigi couldn't stop laughing until she heard the clicking noise again from Hedgie, and she too had a monkey jump on her from behind.

With the monkey still on her back, she asked Hedgie, "How many monkeys are there in this park? I've never seen so many in all the zoos

I've been to."

"There are around five thousand monkeys in this four-acre park. Thailand is known for their great amounts of wild monkeys running around. There are several towns where they just run free, no park at all--like in Loburi."

"What kinds of monkeys are there here?" she asked.

"The two most common types in Thailand are the Macaque monkeys and the Dusty Langurs or leaf monkeys. That one chewing on your hair is a young Macaque, and I think he likes you."

"At least he's better looking than your last boyfriend!" said Justice mockingly.

"He wasn't my boyfriend!" Gigi rebutted. "Be quiet and play with your twin!"

While the bantering continued, they didn't notice the wild-looking monkey rummaging through Justice's golf bag, its clubs now strewn all over the ground. Justice quickly turned to the monkey and shouted "Shoo, shoo, get away!" motioning with his hand. Then before Justice could utter another word, the monkey snatched the driver and streaked off, his little furry tail wagging as he went.

"Oh no, my driver, he's got my driver!" shouted Justice.

The monkey was quickly gaining speed down the path, half carrying the club and half dragging it on the ground. *Out of all the clubs lying on the ground, why in the world did he have to grab that one,* Justice thought to himself.

"Gigi, get your moped. We have to get that little rascal before it's too late!"

"You'll never catch him. He's too fast. Forget about that club, it's gone," said Hedgie, trying to save them from hurting themselves.

"You don't understand, that's my…well…my favorite club. I absolutely have to get it back!"

Then the two sped off on their mopeds, chasing the monkey that was running faster than Prefontaine in a track meet. They were weaving through dozens of furry monkeys that guarded the path ahead. Monkeys were diving furiously into bushes, some leaping over the handle bars, avoiding the recklessly-driven machine that was barreling right toward them.

"Oh no, he's going to ruin the driver. It's scraping across the ground badly!" Justice yelled out.

"Over there. He's trying to drag the driver up that tree. Get him!" shouted Gigi.

Justice jumped off the still moving moped, letting it crash to the ground, and then rushed as fast as he could toward the tree. But it was too late; the monkey had managed to drag the club some fifty feet up the tree. He was smiling down on the two sweaty humans below, holding the driver clumsily in his hands. His wide cheesy grin was the interspecies sign for victory.

"He's too high up. We'll never get him down."

"Let's grab some of these stones. Maybe we can scare him down if we clip him," said Gigi.

The monkey was still smiling, feet dangling back and forth as if he were tap dancing in mid air. Gigi picked up a stone and hurled it towards the monkey, nearly hitting him on the first shot.

Justice joined in, gathering a slew of loose stones from the dirt path. They hurled the stones until their arms grew heavy and weak.

It's no use. We can barely reach him. He's too high up," fumed Gigi.

Just then, perhaps in an act of boredom,

the wild monkey began howling and then jumped down the backside of the mangrove in one fell swoop. The chase was back on! The monkey stopped in mid run, turned around, and was staring right into Justice's frantic eyes. They both were still, staring each other down. It was like an old-fashioned Wild West showdown, pistols drawn and the clock about to strike high noon. The monkey's fur was standing straight up, his hind legs ready to pounce. Justice tiptoed like a ninja towards the monkey, not making a sound. The only thing missing from this face-off was a tumble weed crossing the road. The monkey started swinging the driver above his head, not in an aggressive manner towards Justice, but rather in a warning swing, trying to figure out the purpose of his new heavy toy. There was another white-striped monkey lurking directly behind him, eyeing the new toy himself. Then suddenly the other monkey tackled his fellow compadre, and tried to wrestle the driver out of his hands. The first monkey didn't want to give up his new toy so soon, so he used his legs, kicking wildly to fight off the attacking monkey. He got some distance and decided to use the driver as a caveman club. He swung swiftly and struck the white-striped monkey in the side, causing Justice and Gigi's eyes to widen like saucers, as the next event was something out of a sci-fi comic book.

A bluish spark ignited from the ground, followed by a screeching high-pitched shriek, and the white-striped monkey shot straight into the air like a rocket, past the tallest mangrove in sight and disappeared into the humid sky. A streak of blue light left a trail in the air, and there was a small fire where the monkey had been standing, only a second earlier. The fire was dwindling out as the two regained their senses. They both looked up as far as their vision could allow, and they saw nothing but emptiness. The first monkey dropped the driver and ran for the hills, and Justice was quick to retrieve it. The frayed grip singed his right hand as he reached for it.

"Hey, let's get out of here. This is a bit too bizarre for me," said Gigi.

Just as Justice started to mount his moped,

a howling echoed from above, causing the hairs on his neck to stand straight up.

"Look out!" yelled Gigi.

The white-striped monkey was flying down from the sky like a comet hurtling toward the earth. He was stopped abruptly by a thick mangrove branch about seventy feet up. His fur was almost completely gone, resembling a poodle dog on a bad hair day, and his eyes were as wide as the Grand Canyon. The monkey was trembling so bad, the branch he was perched on was rattling the entire mangrove.

"Gigi, did you see that? He flew in the air for miles. What's happening?"

"I'm not sure, but at least now we know that fishing pole of yours has more powers than just a free flight to Southeast Asia. We need to be very very careful from now on."

They heard the approaching footsteps of Bussra and Hedgie, who finally caught up with them. They were panting and out of breath.

"Are you both all right?" asked Bussra. "Looks like you've seen a ghost."

"Yeah, we're ok." said Gigi. "We got the club back finally. What a relief!"

"If you two are done chasing my monkeys all over the park, I think we should start heading back to my place. It's only a few kilometers away, and it's starting to get dark."

Justice and Gigi grabbed their mopeds and walked back with the other two to the entrance of the gate, realizing how lucky they had been to get that driver back, and avoid a catastrophe.

Hedgie jumped on his bike and led the way out of the park and onto yet another dirty and bumpy path. The sound of monkeys chattering roared in the background and became fainter as they continued farther into the countryside.

CHAPTER SEVEN

H edgie had a straw bungalow in the middle of a small banana plantation. The banana husks formed a barrier around the bungalow, and there wasn't anything else around for miles. They all got off the bikes, took off their shoes, and walked into the largest tree house they had ever seen.

"Wow, this is really cool! You live here all

by yourself? It's like a fort you see in the movies," said Justice.

"It sure is. I built it myself from scratch and planted all those banana trees you see. I grow them for my monkeys at the park. They're much sweeter than the ones you get at the market. My monkeys are too spoiled!"

"I love it here, alone. Gives me time to contemplate life. Well, I'm sure you guys are hungry, so let me whip up some of my special spicy basil chicken."

It didn't take him any time at all to cook the delicious-smelling dinner. They sat on the floor, cross-legged in the meditating lotus position, and devoured the food with earnest.

"So, since all you have with you are your golf clubs and nothing else, I'm assuming you want to go to Bangkok to participate in the annual Thai golf challenge? It's tomorrow, you know."

Justice and Gigi stared at each other and not very convincingly answered, "Uh, yes, yes-- Thai challenge…should be fun. We can't wait."

"This year the winner gets the golden

elephant key which opens the gate to the Majestic Jewel golf course in Chiang Mai."

"Wow, sounds nice. What's so great about that course? Can't we go there without winning anything?" asked Gigi.

"The Majestic Jewel is in the jungle, high in the mountains. It's the most remote course in all of Thailand. Only royalty and the King's family get to play on it."

Justice and Gigi were shaking with excitement.

"That's it, that's the one we need to play on!" Gigi yelled out.

"Well, I hope you brought your "A game" with you from America. Our Thai players are very good and practice for months for this competition. They only allow the first thirty players who sign up to participate, so we'll have to leave right before sunrise."

Hedgie and Bussra cleared the table and then Gigi turned to Justice.

"This is it. We have to win this challenge big brother and play on that course in Chiang

Mai."

"Besides, you're on a roll, champ. I have faith in you, and if you don't win, maybe Hedgie can get us a job at the monkey park. I would give my left arm to see you ride bicycles with a smelly monkey sitting on your head!" chuckled Gigi.

"Very funny, sis. But yes, we absolutely have to win that challenge--no question about it."

Hedgie led Justice and Gigi outside on the deck and pointed to a couple of hammocks that were tied up between two sturdy banana trees. They crawled into the hammock, which swallowed them both like a caterpillar in a cocoon. The stars were the brightest they've ever seen, shining down like miniature spotlights. Crickets were singing a tune in the distance that lulled the two golfers into a deep and undisturbed sleep.

CHAPTER EIGHT

"Rise and shine, kiddos. It's almost 6:00 A.M. Get your clubs, because Hedgie Airlines will be taking off shortly!"

Gigi and Justice slowly crawled out of the hammock, wiped the sleepy crust from their eyes and followed Hedgie to the back of the bungalow where they saw the most ancient-looking sheet of metal with wings. It was painted a banana yellow color, of course. It looked like something out of an old World War II museum, minus the battle scars. Hedgie was trying to crank the propeller, with only a cloud of white smoke coming from the exhaust to show for his effort.

"I think it just needs some more oil. It's been sitting for quite a while."

"Oh great, I think the Red Baron is missing a plane. It will be a miracle if this thing can even get off the ground," said Gigi.

"I hope Hedgie offers flight insurance. I got a bad feeling about this," replied Justice.

Hedgie cranked it one last time after filling it with a couple quarts of oil. The propeller was sputtering, almost coughing, and then surprisingly went into full motion.

"I told you she'd wake up for us--she only needed her morning cup of oil."

They all piled into the banana-colored biplane, barely enough room for everyone. The seats had springs poking through and the door was practically busted. But it started, and that's all that mattered.

"Hang on!" yelled Hedgie.

There was a small strip of dirt path in front of them, carved out of the plantation. The plane gained speed, rattling as it went faster. Hedgie reared back on the steering column, and the plane lifted its nose, clipping a few banana trees as it took off.

"Next stop, Bangkok, kiddos!"

The rumbling of the plane felt like those massage chairs at the mall you can use for a quarter. There were two small windows on each side, which Justice and Gigi had their faces glued to. As the plane gained altitude, they could see the outline of the beach and the massive Andaman Sea. From the air, it was shaped like a boomerang, its curves hugging the edge of the seashore. The hour flight went by quickly, and they were now hovering above Bangkok, staring out at all the ant-sized people moving about chaotically.

"There's the Baiyoke Tower II, the tallest skyscraper in Bangkok, and over there is Lumphini Park. I went boating on the lake last summer. It was a blast," Bussra pointed out.

"Hold on, guys. We need to take a sharp turn. The Thai challenge is on the west bank of the Chao Phraya River. I should be able to get us close."

Hedgie dipped the wings, and the plane dove like a hawk going after a fish in a stream. Justice was starting to lose skin yet again as he held on to his seat and tried to fight off the shade of green his face was turning. The shapes grew larger as they approached, and they both saw the most amazing structure out of the left window of the plane.

"Wow, what's that over there?" Gigi asked Bussra, pointing at the structure on the other side of the massive river.

"That's Wat Arun, or the Temple of Dawn, one of Bangkok's biggest attractions. And that's where you'll be playing today, on the Clawing Tiger golf course. They only open it once a year for this challenge."

The temple was unbelievable and stood apart from anything else in the area. It had a massive elongated tower or *prang,* as the Thais call

it, sticking straight out into the sky, 79 meters high. It's surrounded by four smaller prangs, equally as impressive and decorated by thousands of pieces of multi-colored porcelain. There are over 31,000 Buddhist temples throughout Thailand, Wat Arun being one of the nicest. The plane veered sharply as it dipped away from the tallest prang. Hedgie was definitely flying too close for comfort.

"Thanks for flying Hedgie Airlines. We will be landing shortly. Please put your seats in the upright position," he laughed to himself.

The plane was flying sideways at this point, nearly missing a souvenir tent adjacent to the temple. There was an open field right in front of the temple where Hedgie decided to try to land.

Justice's heart flew up in the ceiling of the plane, as if he were on a roller coaster; the ones he always steered clear of at the Puyallup Fair back home. Gigi was grinning with wild excitement while gnawing off the enamel of her teeth at the same time. The plane's wheels touched down and then took a short hop, like a 2,000-pound frog.

All three of the kids jutted forward, hair standing straight up, but all intact. The plane rested only a few meters away from Wat Arun.

"Come on, grab those clubs and your running legs. We need to hurry if you want to make the cut-off time for signing up. It's almost 7:40," said Hedgie hurriedly.

Justice and Gigi swung the clubs over their shoulders like a sack of potatoes, and they all began to run toward the course. At the opening gate there was a huge yellow banner with red writing that read, *Welcome to the Annual Thai Golf Challenge*, written both in Thai and in English.

CHAPTER NINE

*T*he Clawing Tiger course was like something they'd seen in those golf magazines their dad left around the house, a postcard waiting to be printed. The fairways followed the bend of the Chao Phraya River like a snake. The place was packed with eager young golfers, and there was a short line in front of the sign-up booth. Justice was panting as he approached the clipboard full of names.

"You just made it, young man, with a few minutes to spare. Welcome to the Clawing Tiger," said the man behind the booth. Then he looked directly at Gigi.

"What's your name? And where are you from?"

"I'm Gigi, and this is my brother Justice. He is the one competing today not me. We are from America, Washington State."

"I'm sorry, this year the competition is only for junior girls." He continued on, "Ok, Gigi you are number 30. Wear this sign around your neck, so we know you are one of the competitors. We've never had a foreigner compete in our Thai challenge before. Welcome, and enjoy our course."

Gigi turned to Justice, shaking her head and looking down.

"I haven't really been practicing lately, brother. What are we going to do now?"

"I'm not going to do anything, but you are going to win this thing. Your short game is much better than mine anyway. I'll be your professional caddy this time. At a hundred dollars a day, I'm a bargain."

Hedgie then turned to the kids and said, "It was a pleasure meeting you both. Have fun today, Gigi, and enjoy the rest of Thailand. I should get my plane out of the field before they tow it."

"Thank you so much for the lift and scaring the pants off my big brother during the flight," replied Gigi. "If we ever come back to Phuket, we'll swing by the monkey park and say hello."

Hedgie waved goodbye, and climbed back inside his decrepit plane. The three kids walked over to the rest of the group. There was a huge podium in front of the first hole. A short pudgy man held a microphone, and the other contestants gathered around in a semi circle. Their outfits shining, shoes polished up, this was serious now.

"What's he saying, Bussra?" asked Gigi anxiously.

"Don't worry, I'll translate for you after he's done--also for a small fee of a hundred dollars," Bussra jokingly added.

The man seemed to be talking forever. When he was done, he held up the golden elephant key. The stirring of the contestants stopped as they all stared intently at the key. Then everyone got up and started walking across the first fairway.

"Ok, this is the gist of it, Gigi. There are only three challenges, and he only described the first one so far, which is called the baby-elephant challenge. It's to test your accuracy with your short irons as you try to land your golf ball into the target the elephant is holding--100 yards up to 150 yards away."

"Can you repeat that? It sounded like you said I'll be aiming at a real elephant on the course?" Gigi asked in deep concern.

"This is Thailand, girl. Elephants are our friends here, and they try to make the challenges as creative as possible. Anyway, there will be five elephants, each standing 10 yards behind one another. If you get your ball into the first one, it's worth 1 point, the second one is 3 points, the third one is 5 points, the next one is 7 points and the last elephant is worth 10 points. Only the top four scores will move onto the next challenge."

"And if we hit the elephant with a golf ball, and we upset him, we lose and run for our life, right?"

"Not exactly, silly. You will be using yellow foam practice balls, but they fly just as far. Most Thais are Buddhists, and we don't believe in ever hurting animals, especially something as big as an elephant."

"The first challenge starts on hole number 10. Come on, we need to catch up with the others."

As they approached the 10th hole, they immediately noticed the baby elephants playing with each other and rolling around in the middle of the fairway. They were each wearing a different colored headdress--laced with gold, blue sapphires, and red gems.

There was an older gentleman dressed in a white, button-down suit and shiny steel-tipped black shoes. He was the one directing the contestants to their positions. He put them in three rows of ten players, Gigi being in the final row on account of her arriving late and getting #30. The spectators were flooding in, hovering around the hole to cheer on their favorite player.

The man in the white suit clapped his hands twice, and the elephants immediately lined up into their positions. The first one was wearing a green headdress, exactly 100 yards away, and the other four walked backwards in unison, until the last elephant stood 150 yards away. There were two young helpers near the elephants, holding some ornate-looking vases with caricatures of various animals on them. One by one the baby elephants picked up the vases in their trunks.

"The elephants follow instructions better than half of my 4th grade class. It's amazing!" laughed Gigi.

"What are the vases for?"

"That's what you have to land your golf ball into. It's really tough. The opening of the vase is no bigger than that dinner plate Hedgie served the basil chicken on last night."

"I think the games at the Puyallup Fair are much easier than this. And I never come away with a prize there. Look, the elephants are moving the vases up and down with their trunks. I'll be lucky to even make one ball inside. Now I'm really nervous."

"Don't worry. You only have to make the top four. Just don't blow it."

"Gee, thanks. That really took all the pressure off!"

The first ten contestants took their place on the white chalk line right in front of the tee mat along with their golf balls. The contestants were taking a few practice hits, and yellow balls were flying everywhere, covering the fairway like wild daisies. The director motioned towards them, and then the first challenge was underway.

The second girl to tee off was really taking her time compared to the first contestant, checking for wind and everything. She struck her third ball, and as it travelled near the last elephant 150 yards away, the crowd roared with excitement. Her ball hit the back lip of the ornate vase and rolled in! She jumped up and down and then took a ceremonial bow to the crowd and tipped her bright pink golf hat. 10 points! Her next attempt sailed to the right of the first elephant, but the last ball flew directly into the third elephant's vase, scoring her another 5 points.

"The girl in the pink hat is on fire! 15 points might be the top score of her group," commented Gigi.

"The director will post the scores from the first group on the leader board over there," explained Bussra. "A few others have scored high as well, but 15 will be hard to beat."

The first group was almost finished. The wind began picking up, coming in from the river, making Gigi's nervous little arms shake even more. The director climbed up a small staircase behind the scoreboard and started putting in the scores one at a time. Sure enough, 15 was the top score. The second highest score was 10, and the rest ranged from 5 points to 3 points, and two contestants didn't even score one point.

The second group took their place, yielding much of the same results. The wind was making it very difficult to get an accurate ball flight, not to mention the elephants were becoming restless and moving the vases around more, so the yellow balls were hitting everything but the vases. Then suddenly the crowd roared again, as one player sunk her ball into the target 140 yards away. 7 points! Her next shot appeared to be going in also.

"Oh no, this isn't looking too good for me. That girl just made another ball in the second elephant's vase for another 3 points!" Gigi cried out.

Soon, the second group was all done, and the director was climbing up that tiny staircase again. Gigi's heart was pounding, as she noticed that two players scored 12 in the second group, followed by the girl who just made 10, and two others managed to get 8 points.

"Ok, you're up, sis. Remember what our golf teacher, Mr. Coleman, taught us about the short iron swing. Head down, short back swing, and don't forget to follow through. And open the face a little bit," instructed Justice.

"I remember, but it's a little different swinging the ball at a bunch of elephants holding porcelain vases," chuckled Gigi.

"Gigi, you need at least 12 points to get into the next challenge. You can do this!" encouraged Bussra.

Justice handed her the 9 iron to start with.

Gigi laced up her shoes tightly, stretched out her back, and took her spot on the mat. This was it. *No turning back now,* she thought. The wind was swirling harder, and the fear of not being able to hit even one vase sunk deep into the pit of her stomach. She was in the sixth position and patiently awaited her turn. She placed the little yellow ball right in the middle of her stance. She adjusted her grip, brought the 9 iron back and then took her first swing. The ball sliced to the right and didn't even travel to the first elephant, 100 yards away.

"Come on, put a little mustard on it!" Justice shouted from behind the tee.

Gigi placed the second ball more parallel with her front foot, hoping to add a little distance. She swung again, this time with more determination. The ball flight was straight; she got a lot of launch and followed all the way through, with the end of the club resting behind her back. The yellow streak flew past the first elephant, then the second, it was heading directly towards the third elephant. *Come on, come on,* she repeated to herself. The ball hit the elephant on the side of the head, took an awkward bounce and somehow managed to find the lip of the porcelain vase and settled in.

Gigi clenched her fist and shook it above her head. She finally was able to relax and let out a sly smile. The elephant let out a loud trumpeting noise, as if to say, *congratulations, you just scored 5 points!* Her jubilation was short lived, however, as her next ball sailed to the right again, coming up short of the third elephant. It came down to her last ball--one last try.

"Focus. You need to hit the fourth elephant at 140 yards for 7 points, or you're finished!" yelled Justice.

"Pass me the 8 iron, Justice. There's no way I can reach it with my 9 iron, with the wind and all," Gigi shouted back.

Justice slid through the crowd and handed her the club. The wind was picking up, and her heart was beating through her chest like a steam locomotive. She placed her last yellow ball on the mat. Only one other golfer in her group made it into the vase at 110 yards, so it was up to her to win or lose this challenge. She took a couple practice swings to calm down, and now the time had come. Head down, feet firmly planted, game on! She made solid contact in the sweet spot of the yellow ball; unfortunately, it was sailing to the right again. It had the distance, but this competition looked to be over for her. But a gust of wind suddenly came off the Chao Phraya River, re-steering her ball towards the last elephant. This could be the break she needed. The crowd's eyes stuck to her ball like glue, and they began cheering when the ball inched closer to the last elephant. Another gust of wind stopped the ball flight in mid air, and it started falling directly toward the fourth elephant. It clanked against the left edge of the vase, bounced up in the air a few feet, and dropped into the bottom of the vase. Gigi dropped her 8 iron and put her hands in front of her face in a gesture of shock. Bussra and Justice came running up behind her, nearly knocking her to the ground.

"I can't believe it, sis! That gust of wind

came at the perfect time!"

"Yeah, I timed that gust perfectly, haha. Well, I hope I don't need that much luck to win the next challenge. That was a bit too intense for me!"

CHAPTER TEN

*T*he crowd was pointing at Gigi, giving her the thumb's up, and some even offering a second thumb for extra measure. The girl in the pink hat was walking towards Gigi, her hand outstretched.

"Good shot! My name is Karis. I've never golfed with a foreigner before. I wish you good luck today."

Gigi introduced herself, and then Karis rejoined her family. Now the competition was narrowed down to four. So, just like that, the rest of the contestants were put into early retirement, slumping away. The announcer was making his way to the tee mats, shaking hands with the remaining four. He held a cordless microphone, and began speaking in Thai to them. Gigi looked bewildered, wondering what the next wild challenge could possibly be. Then her translating savior, Bussra, came up beside her.

"Great job, Gigi. Wow, you passed your first skills challenge, and you're into the second round. That's terrific! Now the next challenge is a driving competition, over a 200-yard lake. You need to avoid two streams coming off the waterfall about 350 yards away. It's the best of two balls, real ones this time. We need to get to the 14th tee. They'll start soon."

Gigi took a big gulp, the look of defeat plastered her face.

"Hey, what's wrong, girl? You should be celebrating your first round advancement."

Justice answered for her: "She doesn't hit long off the tee at all. I've never seen her drive it past 190 yards, even in perfect summer conditions."

"Oh, well maybe the other three girls can't drive it long either. Don't worry so much."

"Thanks, but it was fun while it lasted, I guess," replied Gigi sullenly.

The three of them walked quickly towards the 14th hole. Gigi joined the other three competitors on the tee box, staring down the daunting lake, which to her might as well have been the Red Sea. The waterfall was enormous, and its crashing sounds could be heard all the way from the tee mats.

Karis was first to tee off. Her swing form was almost flawless, and she ripped one past the lake, in between the two streams, 220 yards away. The next girl didn't have a fast swing speed, but her golf ball travelled far, flying low, landing around 210 yards. Her ball continued to roll, looking as if she might take the lead, but then it suddenly took a dive into the stream. She sighed

and walked sluggishly off the mat. It was Gigi's turn now. She hesitantly took her old driver from her bag, placed her golf ball on the tee, which was set low, shifted her hips and swung down. Sure enough, the ball lost its wings around 175 yards, and splashed into the lake. She slapped her leg in anger, as her ball caused a rippling effect in the still water. It was all over, and she knew it. The final girl also had a smooth swing and smacked it past the 220 mark. It stopped rolling around 240 yards, and she was currently the new leader.

The players took a drink of water and prepared for round two of the long-drive contest. Karis had a fierce look on her face, her eyes dialed in down the fairway. She took a full swing at her second ball, her body contorting as she followed through. It had a low trajectory, and cut through the wind like a butter knife. It touched down around 230 yards and took a generous hop, past 240, and finally stopped at 250 yards! The other two teed off before Gigi this time, but failed short of Karis' heroic 250-yard drive. Gigi had a crazy look in her eye, and she lunged for Justice's golf bag and pulled out the dangerous driver before he could even react.

"Wait, are you crazy! Nooooooo!" screamed Justice.

"It's the only way, brother. We have to win this. We don't have any other choice!"

Before he could answer, Gigi hurried back to the tee box. Her hands were shaking in anticipation of what might happen next. She could barely steady her hand enough to put the tee in the soft ground. She was careful to swing quickly, trying not to think about anything and to leave all pure thoughts hanging in the breeze. The high pitched ringing sound could be heard throughout the crowd as she connected with her ball. Gigi dropped the driver and had to cover her own ears from the blistering sound. Justice covered his ears as well, his face showing absolute frustration.

The ball tore through the air, moving faster than a cheetah chasing after its prey. There was a faint blue streak that left a trail from the ball, a small fire ignited on the ground, and Gigi was quick to stomp it out. The ball was travelling so fast that it shed its outer urethane cover as it flew past the lake. The blue streak continued to leave its mark in the sky as it was still airborne, flying over the fairway, past the two streams and pierced into the waterfall, shedding its second layer at impact. The ringing finally ceased and the astonished faces of all those who saw the ball leave the tee box were transfixed on the waterfall.

"Holy smokes. If her ball hadn't crashed into the waterfall, it might have gone 500 yards!" Karis pointed out.

Gigi turned white as the sand at Maya Bay and began sweating profusely. She wiped her brow and had to gather herself quickly.

"It's all in the hips, and that gust of wind must have helped."

"There wasn't any wind at all when you teed off!" remarked Karis suspiciously.

"Didn't you feel…?" Gigi tried to answer.

The silence broke as a few people in the crowd yelled and shouted wildly, setting off a wave of loud cheers. Justice and Bussra came around to the front of the tee box. Justice was grinding his teeth, his face knotted in anger. Bussra was congratulating Gigi and raising her hand in the air.

"How'd you do that? I've never seen anybody hit a golf ball that far."

"Like I said, it's all in the hips!"

Justice grabbed Gigi by her arm, faking his smile and pulled her to the side.

"That wasn't funny. You could have gotten us into a lot of trouble. You're lucky we're not standing in the middle of a glacier somewhere in Siberia right now! If your ball hadn't smashed into the waterfall, it would've gone another mile."

"I'm so sorry, I wasn't thinking about anything pure when I struck the ball though. I panicked. Kinda stupid, I guess."

"Please, sis, we've got to be very careful with this club. Don't ever pull another stunt like that again, ok?"

"I promise, but did you see my drive? Sign me up for the LPGA, brother!" laughed Gigi.

There was an elderly man in a blue suede

suit, holding a microphone, approaching Gigi and
Karis.

"That's the owner of the golf course. His
English is quite good. I think he's going to
announce the final challenge," said Bussra.

He stood in between the two girls, and
began speaking in Thai at first, and then in
English.

"Please put your hands together for our
two finalists! The last challenge that will
determine the winner of the golden key will be the
Bengal Tiger challenge. These competitors will
have three chances to land their golf ball into the
mouth of the tiger statue that stands sixty feet
high."

The man seemed very excited to practice
his English, especially in front of such a large
group of people. He stepped down off the
podium and waved to the crowd as they all began
marching behind him, like mice following the
fiddler. Karis turned to Gigi and spoke timidly.

"You are a great player. You hit the ball so
far!"

Then she reached into her bag and pulled out a brand new golf glove.

"Here, you can have this. I saw you struggling with yours. Mine is much smaller, should fit better."

Gigi looked amazed. Her competition was trying to help her. What a great show of sportsmanship. She let out a humble thank you and they began walking together to the 17th hole.

CHAPTER ELEVEN

*T*he entire tee box was covered with red carpet and two white tee mats placed beside each other. The three yellow practice balls were in a small ceramic cup next to the mats. About fifty yards away stood the towering 60-foot tiger statue which was surrounded by a chain-linked fence and a wooden track that went 360 degrees around the tiger's head. The tiger's mouth was wide open, its teeth made of stone-washed marble. The crowd soon gathered around the hole. Justice and Bussra were marveling at the statue in awe. Suddenly a loud roar escaped from behind the statue's gigantic head, and everyone jumped back in shock.

"And what's a tiger challenge, without real Bengal Tigers!" The owner chuckled.

Just then two monstrous tigers emerged from behind the statue, prancing around the wooden track and clawing at the marble teeth. Their markings were magnificent, white and yellow stripes flowing from their faces to their backs. One tiger was much larger than the other and had a deeper growl. They were as elegant as they were frightening.

"To make the last challenge more interesting, we placed a salmon in the back of the statue's mouth, a tiger's favorite appetizer. The two finalists must avoid the swinging claws if they want their ball to make it into the mouth."

"Great! First, baby elephants with fast moving trunks, and now real tigers. This sure

beats the miniature golf course we played near the
Hoh River campground. I thought the moving
windmill and clown face were tough!" said Gigi.

"It's all about timing. Take your time and
wait for the tiger to stop swinging his paws before
you swing. Just don't jump off the mat when he
roars," said Justice.

The owner reached out and grabbed Gigi's shoulder and led her to the center of the red carpet to join Karis. He had a small silver coin in his palm and asked Gigi to call it. She said tails. *As the old saying goes,* she thought, *tails never fails.* He flipped the coin, it rotated several times in the air and spun on the carpet before finally landing on…heads. Karis elected to go first.

"Good luck to you, and thanks again for the new glove. My friends back home wouldn't give me a snow shovel in a blizzard, if we were competing."

"My pleasure. I hope we can be friends when this is over. That's more important than the key anyway."

Gigi nodded, and Karis took her place on the mat. They were only allowed to use their 56-degree sand wedge, a club that Gigi was actually quite comfortable with. Karis squared her legs over the first ball, glanced up at the tiger's mouth and hit it flush. The Bengal tigers were clawing vigorously now, determined to get a piece of salmon that tempted their taste buds. Her ball shot left of the head. The larger tiger tried to swipe at it, but only caught air instead. She only missed the target by a couple of feet. Karis lined up her second ball closer to the right side of the mat, peered intensely at the roaming tigers and took another smooth swing at the ball. It was heading straight for the savage mouth. The crowd let out a collective gasp, as the ball avoided the tiger's claws as if it had eyes, and bounced off the front marble teeth and rolled inside. Karis was jumping ecstatically in the air; this might have been the final dagger in the competition. She was too excited to even concentrate on her final attempt, which flew right over the statue altogether. It didn't matter though, one point should be enough to seal the deal. Gigi congratulated her and reached down and grabbed her first yellow ball.

"You got this, sis. Pretend the tigers are fluffy bunnies or something--just ignore them."

She looked back with a wry smile; it would take another miracle to pull off the victory. She looked down at her ball, almost in a trance, waited for the tigers to settle down, and started her swing motion. As the club hit the apex on her backswing, the smaller tiger let out a hideous roar, and Gigi jumped a little and completely shanked her ball about ten yards toward the crowd. This wasn't a good start--not at all. She was still trembling as she placed the second ball back on the mat and waited. She took another solid swing, this time with no interruption. She didn't get under the ball enough, and it travelled with too much juice on it, landing right next to Karis' last attempt.

It all came down to this: one last yellow ball and a statue surrounded by two hungry tigers. Gigi sighed, closed her eyes and let it fly. It was heading slightly left, but started to turn on a direct path to the mouth. The distance looked good, and she prayed for another lucky shot to go her way. It was on a laser beam line, aimed at the center of the statue's mouth. It was going in…it was i… Just then the larger tiger leaped towards the ball, swinging his paw at the shiny yellow object-blaam! He struck it in mid flight and shredded it in half.

You have to be kidding me, Gigi thought. Her stomach sank to the ground, and she dropped her head in disappointment. There was no other chance; the tiger got the best of her. It was all over. She lost. Justice pushed his way through the rambunctious crowd, wanting to be the first to console his defeated sister.

"If it makes you feel any better, I wouldn't even have made it out of the first round. We'll figure out another way to get home. You did all you could," he said.

The owner was back on the microphone. He had both his hands behind his back, as he spoke to the excited crowd.

"Congratulations to both of the players. You put up a good fight, and I didn't want to see either of you lose. Gigi, as our first foreign competitor, you showed us strength and courage-- that of a Bengal Tiger. So, it is my honor to present both of you with a golden key and an invitation to play at the prestigious Majestic Jewel at your own leisure in Chiang Mai."

The two girls slapped hands and were

practically dancing out of their golf shoes. Since they could use the golden key anytime they wanted, it was uncertain if their paths would cross again. The moment was now, the celebration was now, and they were embracing it. Gigi truly couldn't believe the good news she had just heard. She accepted the key and the tears were rolling more steadily…tears of joy.

The owner reached out for Gigi again and was assuming the picture-posing position. Cameras were flashing from all different angles. The man in the white suit also joined the posing party along with a few of the spectators. They were all eager to introduce themselves to Gigi and smile bright for the cameras.

"Hey, celebrity. We should get going. Chiang Mai awaits us, wherever that might be," said Justice.

Bussra jumped in: "It's in Northern Thailand, you guys, almost 9 hours away. Not sure how we're going to get there. It's an awful long walk."

CHAPTER TWELVE

*T*hey began walking towards that large yellow banner with red lettering that welcomed them in to this wild competition, not knowing where to go or how to get there. Wat Arun was shimmering in the distance, its towers twinkling in the sunlight. As they got closer they could see the intricate details, and the porcelain figurines that were sculpted more than two hundred years ago. It was mesmerizing and washed away any worries they had. The crowd was filing out quickly behind them, like a herd of buffalo, and the voices of chattering people seemed to fuse together, all except for one.

"Anybody see a monkey flying the Red Baron's plane around here?" yelled a familiar voice from afar.

Gigi was the first to turn around, and noticed Hedgie, poking his head out from the crowd of moving voices.

"Hedgieee, great to see you!" said Gigi in sheer surprise. "I thought you had to get back to the monkey park?"

"I was about to take off when I heard all the excitement going on. I decided my monkeys could fend for themselves another day. Besides, I hear you need a lift to Chiang Mai. Congratulations, little lady!"

"Thanks, Hedgie. You're a life saver. I don't see the yellow banana anywhere. Maybe someone ate it."

"I moved it, just on the other side of Wat Arun. The parking meter was about to expire," chuckled Hedgie.

They walked over to the plane and crawled inside, all eager to get to Chiang Mai, except for Justice who was already turning lettuce-green. He was standing outside the rusty door of the plane.

"Nine hours by bus, right? If I jog, I could be there in a few days. Catch you later," he said.

Gigi softly punched him in the stomach and dragged him in by his shirt collar. Soon they were off, and being veterans of the flying business now, they weren't half as scared as the first flight. They flew low over the massive Chao Phraya River and over the busy, building-ridden Bangkok. Gigi had the golden key resting in her lap, and she was stroking it like she would her kitty, Rocky, back home. The purring was replaced by the sounds of roaring tigers and howling baby elephants. *What a day this has been,* she thought to herself, *what a day.*

The three of them fell into nap mode during the flight, and before they knew it, they could feel the plane dip its wings and descend from the clouds. Mountains painted the landscape below, and they prepared for yet another open-field landing.

"Kids, this may be bumpier than our first landing, but I think I can avoid the mountains."

"You think…you think! I told you I should have jogged here!" Justice exclaimed.

They touched down, and the plane took its familiar frog hop--not one this time, but several whiplashing hops. Hedgie pulled up on the brake, and the plane came to a screeching halt. Justice quickly opened the hatch and laid face first in the field, kissing the ground he had missed so badly.

"Everyone all right? That was a rough one. It's nearly five o'clock already, so you'll have to visit the Majestic Jewel tomorrow. It'll be dark by the time we get there."

"I know a great night bazaar in town. I vote we all go and get some local food for dinner. I'm starving," Hedgie said, his stomach growling.

The three began crossing the field toward the road. The walk was refreshing, and helped to shake the queasiness they got from another inventive Hedgie Airlines' landing.

CHAPTER THIRTEEN

*T*hey reached the road, and Hedgie was flagging down two moving objects that looked like Justice's school lunch pail with three wheels and an engine.

"What in the world is that supposed to be?" asked Gigi.

"It's a tuk tuk, Thailand's most convenient and popular way to get around. Hop in--it won't bite you," answered Bussra.

Justice and Gigi got into the one behind Hedgie's, and the tuk tuks sped off like a go-cart on a race track--a far cry from their dad's old station wagon that moved about as fast as a grandma in a rocking chair on a hot summer's day. They cruised down the road at warp speed and eventually got to the main city area and to the Royal Market the locals called *Kad Luang*. It was a night bazaar located right on the Ping River, and there were hundreds of stalls selling everything from CD's to exotic types of street food. The food vendors' English wasn't too great, but they smiled joyfully and pointed at their goods uttering a "you try" or "cheap price today." They were grilling behind their mini mobile kitchens, and the smell of barbeque smoke filled the air.

"You guys ever try *takatan tod*, fried crickets? They're delicious--tastes like potato chips with an extra crunch," laughed Bussra.

"You're kidding, right? I flicked them off my dad's station wagon windshield before, but never had any desire to dip them in ranch and eat them!" replied Gigi.

"Come on, they are considered a scrumptious treat in Southeast Asia. Just try one. If crickets aren't your thing, there are fried grasshoppers and ants as well."

"Ok, I'll try one cricket, only if Justice eats one too."

Justice eventually agreed after some forceful persuasion, and they plopped a cricket each into their mouths. Justice had his eyes closed and was chewing as fast as he could. They made the final gulp, and down the hatch the crickets went.

"Not so bad, I guess. Tastes like mom's homemade french fries," Justice said with a sour look on his face.

Bussra and Hedgie laughed, and they led the two cricket warriors through the many rows of the Royal Market. They got a plate of fresh papaya salad and feasted on some *pla-meuk yang*-- grilled squid on a stick. They sat at a table, facing the Ping River and watched the numerous shoppers milling around.

"Hope you got enough to eat. We should be heading out soon. It's getting late, and those don't look too friendly," Hedgie said, pointing at the ominous clouds above.

"I have a buddy who has a cottage near the Borichinda Cave, below the Doi Inthanon Mountain. It's the highest mountain in all of Thailand and where the Majestic Jewel is located. I'm sure we can stay with him."

"Sounds far away. Another tuk tuk ride is in our future, I figure?" asked Justice.

Before Hedgie could answer, the rain started pouring down in torrential fashion, hitting the streets like a sledgehammer, leaving not a single space between drops. The vendors ran for cover and set up their huge umbrellas. Shoppers scurried everywhere, searching for a dry, covered spot. Hedgie took off, back towards the street, holding his dinner plate over his head. Justice and the girls followed close behind, lugging their rain-filled golf bags. In a matter of minutes, they were already drenched to the bone. They saw the two tuk tuk drivers and jumped into the torn leather seats, escaping the pelting drops.

"How do you like our Thai rainfall? It should stop in a few minutes. It's like a free shower," Hedgie yelled back to Justice and Gigi who were shivering and wringing out their clothes.

"Well, it sure beats the heat, but I forgot my bar of soap!" Gigi cackled back.

Hedgie started cracking up, and the tuk

tuks were off and rolling again. Sure enough, the rain had begun to lighten up a couple minutes later, and the road ahead was clear. They were heading straight out of town, and zigzagging up a steep hill. Civilization was in the rearview mirror, which was slowly disappearing in the distance. A vibrant rainbow started to surface out of the raindrops, spanning across the fields and stretching out toward the alluring Doi Inthanon Mountain.

CHAPTER FOURTEEN

*T*he rugged tuk tuk ride seemed to take forever, and they finally arrived at the wooden rustic cottage. The air was much cooler there, a great escape from the humidity of the bustling city. The cave was just on the other side of a small stream that flowed out of the entrance that ran by the cottage. The four hopped out, and Hedgie was greeted by his friend, who must have heard them coming a mile away. He was much older than Hedgie, but carried his age well. His real name was Proddick, but all his buddies called him Leonard. They chatted awhile, and Hedgie turned back and gave a thumbs up to the kids.

"No problem. He has room for all of us. And you don't have to sleep in a hammock this time," he called out.

Leonard led them into the cottage and into a small room in the back and put their golf clubs on the bunk beds. He was very shy to try out his English, so Hedgie kept him company while the kids ran out the door, wanting to explore the cave.

"Wait!" yelled Leonard in his crackly voice. "Try these--too dark."

He tossed three headlamps their way, and they strapped them on tightly and walked swiftly toward the cave. Bussra helped Justice and Gigi turn on their high beams as they entered the opening.

The cave was dark and damp. The headlamps flickered, and they started to follow the stream that ran calmly through the middle.

Gigi pointed at the ceiling and asked, "What are those sharp objects poking out the top of the cave. They won't fall on us, will they?"

"No, we're safe from falling objects here. Those are stalactites--limestone spires. They're not going anywhere," replied Bussra.

The bobbing lights continued up through the cave. It was becoming a lot darker towards the back, and cooler as well. Goosebumps were forming on Gigi's little arms. They stuck close together, maneuvering through the loose rocks and dark spots. A cooing noise came from the ceiling, and then the sound of wings flapping came rushing towards Justice, who was slightly ahead of the girls. He dove face first on the ground, his arms splashing in the stream.

"Bat! A bat tried to attack me! I'm outta here!" he cried.

He scrambled past the girls, nearly knocking them into the stream. The flying creature was making a second attempt at Justice, circling him like a raven. The girls were laughing at this point, but also weary of this unidentified flying object and began running after Justice, towards the light and out of the darkness. They reached the opening of the cave, and the creature flew directly over their heads, landing on a tree branch. They all got a better glimpse at Justice's attacker.

"That's not a bat, silly boy. It's a Chinese flying squirrel. He's harmless," said Bussra.

The girls began laughing like hyenas. Justice flushed from embarrassment, and marched off back to the cottage, stomping his feet in irritation.

"Hey Justice, didn't know you were so famous with the squirrel population. I think you two would make a cute couple!" laughed Gigi.

The girls caught up with Justice, poking him and rousing him all the way back to the cottage. When they walked inside, Hedgie and Leonard were playing cards on the dining room table. The kids took off their headlamps and thanked Leonard for his hospitality.

"How was the cave, girls? It gets pretty dark inside, huh?" asked Hedgie.

"It was pretty cool, and Justice made a new friend!" said Gigi laughing hysterically again.

"Well, you must be exhausted from the long day we've all had. Your bunks are made up already, so I'll see you in the morning."

They said their pleasant goodnights,

crawled into the bunks and fell into dreamland, listening to the restless sounds outside their window. The rain began to thunder down again, quieting the jungle and tucking it in for the night.

CHAPTER FIFTEEN

Morning came quickly. The kids staggered out of their bunks and into the living room. Leonard was frying up some scrambled eggs and offered them some fresh coconut juice and handpicked mangos.

"So, are you two excited about being able to use that golden key finally?" asked Bussra.

"Can't wait to see this course. When are we

all leaving?" replied Justice.

"I'm sorry, kids. I really need to get back to Phuket today. My monkeys must be going crazy already."

Bussra looked sadly at Hedgie.

"I'm afraid I need to be going too. My dad is probably making missing posters of me by now. I would stay if I could."

Justice and Gigi embraced them both, not able to say thank you enough times. Hedgie was worried about leaving them alone, but Justice reassured him that they could manage by themselves.

"We've arranged for your ride up to the golf course. It's only nine kilometers from here through the jungle. It rained most of the night, so you wouldn't be able to walk there anyway," said Hedgie.

They sat down in the living room, in an awkward silence and finished the rest of their mangos. Gigi reached around her neck and unsnapped her favorite hand-woven necklace. It was given to her by her late grandfather when she was four, and she never ever took it off. She graciously handed it to Bussra.

"When you wear this necklace, please think of us and this crazy adventure we've had together. I'll never forget you," said Gigi, tears forming in her eyes.

The crying was broken up by the thundering noise coming from right outside the cottage. Justice and Gigi recognized the loud trumpeting sound...it couldn't be.

"Your chariots await, my dear friends!" Hedgie said excitedly.

They opened the door and saw two colossal elephants standing tall and waving their trunks, as if to say hello. A wooden seat wrapped in a green satin cloth rested on their backs. The young man steering the lovely giant clapped his hands, and the two elephants knelt down simultaneously.

"Don't keep your ride waiting. Go ahead and climb aboard," Bussra said.

They both mounted the elephants, holding on firmly to the small leather handle attached to

JASON T. ROSS

the chair. They rose up together, and Justice and Gigi were now sitting ten feet above the ground. Gigi sat behind the young trainer, and Justice was riding solo close behind.

"Sure beats my Hedgie Airlines, I bet!"

"I won't be getting any frequent flyer miles on this guy though," Gigi said while scratching the elephant behind his ear.

The young trainer clapped again, and the two gray giants began marching off. Justice and Gigi waved back at their friends until they could no longer see them. The elephants made their way through the dense jungle, one giant step at a time. They came across a small flowing waterfall a couple kilometers ahead. The base was covered with white wild orchids and jagged rocks. Tropical birds were chirping along the ride, and unfamiliar animal noises were everywhere.

It was much cooler today than it had been when they arrived yesterday. The frosty morning mist blanketed the jungle, and the sunlight was trying to get its first glimpse of the day. The steam began to rise from the path they trampled on as

they passed the waterfall and started heading
directly up the slippery slope of the mountain.
Through the fog, they could see a massive gate,
made entirely out of crystal, its reflection almost
blinding.

"Oh my goodness. Justice we're here. This
is it, brother!"

The elephants knelt down outside the gate,

and Justice and Gigi slid down their side, stumbling onto the path. They shook the young trainer's hand and bowed their heads out of respect. The entrance gate was almost a block long, and decorated with gold and silver flakes. The door was hand carved out of mahogany wood, and there was a huge key hole, in the shape of an elephant.

"Go ahead, sis, try your key. I can't believe we made it here in one piece."

She carefully put the key in the hole. It took both of her hands to turn it until she heard the loud clicking noise. Then the door slowly swung open. They walked toward the clubhouse, taking in the views of this secluded and serene course when they were startled by a tall, grizzly man with a low baritone voice.

"I'm sorry, we are closed today. The greens are soaked from the heavy rains last night. Nobody can play on them for the next few days. How'd you get in anyway?" he asked.

The whole world came crashing down on Gigi and Justice in that single second. All the travelling and hard work getting here was for nothing. Gigi held up the golden elephant key, which was useless to her at this point. The begging process was now in effect.

"Please sir, we came a very long way. Is there any chance we can just play one hole? We promise not to stomp on anything," she pleaded.

The grizzly man was very reluctant, but finally gave in to Gigi's innocent, batting eyes.

"Oh, ok, ok. You can play a couple of holes, but then you'll have to come back some other time. You can tee off on hole number 3 over there, its fairway isn't drowning as bad as the others."

CHAPTER SIXTEEN

*T*he hole was situated overlooking the bluff of the mountain on an elevated tee box. The views were breathtaking, and they could see all the way down the valley and even a stretch of the Ping River. The sign post was made of dark green jade, and the number 3 was written with white diamonds. Two red rhododendron bushes marked the back tees clearly.

"So, big brother, what do you say we finish what we started back home? I would've won, you know."

"You're on! Would you care to make a friendly wager on this hole? The loser has to feed Rocky for the next two months, including those 4:00 A.M. wake-up calls, if and when we ever get home," replied Justice.

"It's a bet, and don't start whining when Rocky pounces on you all hours of the night for her tuna feast. Now we'll see who will wear the family crown!"

Justice reached for his 3 wood and was first to tee off on this dogleg left par 4. He gripped it and ripped it, his ball running far down the left edge of the fairway. Gigi used her driver, got some good distance herself, but landed well behind Justice. They grabbed their golf bags, took one last glance at the valley below and wandered after their tee shots. The fairway was lined with hundreds of artistically pruned roses, and the grass looked like it had been hand cut by scissors, with not one divot in sight. The dew draped over the evergreen trees nestled in the forest, and the pecking of a few white-bellied woodpeckers echoed rhythmically. Gigi found her slightly frozen ball through the thick morning mist. She pulled out her 4 iron and swung for the fences.

"Good shot. I guess it's a little easier to concentrate when you're not aiming at baby elephants waving vases at you!"

Gigi laughed and watched her ball sink into the water-logged grass about forty yards from the green, which was actually a small island guarded by a rather large moat. Justice had a good lie, and was close enough to use his faithful 7 iron. Just as he was about to swing, they heard a rustling noise coming from the other side of the fairway. Justice froze in astonishment as he saw what emerged from the dew-drenched forest: a young Asiatic Black Bear. It let out a tiny growl and was staring at the two shivering golfers. Its shaggy ears were fairly large, and it wore a white crescent-shaped mark on its chest.

"Don't move a muscle, brother. It won't bother us if we don't bother him," Gigi whispered, recalling an episode she saw on the Animal Planet channel. And the black bear did just that; it turned around and walked up to the ceramic fountain spewing from the moat and began lapping up the water. Justice was still shaking as he was about to swing, waiting for the bear to take his last sip, and head back to the forest.

"Now you know how I felt swinging at those Bengal Tigers," heckled Gigi. "Who's laughing now?"

His nerves took control of his body, and he chunked his golf ball, hitting it fat, and it landed almost parallel with Gigi's own ball, missing an easy chance to putt for the win.

"Nice one, buddy! How about we play closest to pin from here for the family bragging rights? I think my hands are too cold to make a steady putt anyway," said Gigi.

They shook in agreement, and Justice let Gigi go first. Using her 60-degree lob wedge, she hit it crisp, getting under her ball, adding some serious spin. It landed past the pin, and spun back within five to six feet from the hole. She was ecstatic, slugging Justice in his arm and taunting him as he prepared for his attempt. He also hit his ball high, watching it spin in slow motion through the air. It landed short, but was still rolling, kicking up moisture as it went. It stopped on the opposite side of Gigi's ball, also only a few feet from the hole.

"Yes!" Justice yelled out, poking back at Gigi.

"I call it a draw, brother. You got lucky this time!" Gigi said in dismay.

They fist-bumped each other, crossed the tiny cobblestone bridge of the moat, and picked up their balls. They sauntered over to the next hole, basking in the natural beauty that encompassed them.

****

The mist was still dancing off the fairway, and the sunlight was now wide awake and smiling. Justice methodically pulled the magic driver out of his golf bag and looked across at Gigi. It was time to go...and they both knew it. He reluctantly placed his icy Spreeline on the tee, closed his eyes, and fell silent. As he struck his ball, the familiar deafening sound came alive and took its final breath in Thailand...and they disappeared into the unknown...leaving only their shadows behind, on the misty mountain top of this enchanted country.

Visit our website to learn more about **Justice and Gigi's World Golf Adventures** at
www.themagicdriver.com

CPSIA information can be obtained at www.ICGtesting.com

224377LV00001B/1/P